Jack!

Hey Jack! Books

First American Edition 2020
Kane Miller, A Division of EDC Publishing
Original Title: Hey Jack: Star of the Week
Text Copyright © 2015 Sally Rippin
Illustration Copyright © 2015 Stephanie Spartels
Logo and Design Copyright © 2015 Hardie Grant Egmont
First published in Australia by Hardie Grant Egmont

For information contact:
Kane Miller, A Division of EDC Publishing
P.O. Box 470663
Tulsa, OK 74147-0663
www.kanemiller.com
www.edcpub.com
www.usbornebooksandmore.com

Library of Congress Control Number: 2019951218

Printed and bound in the United States of America
1 2 3 4 5 6 7 8 9 10
ISBN: 978-1-68464-134-5

The Star
of the
Week

By Sally Rippin

Illustrated by Stephanie Spartels

Kane Miller

A DIVISION OF EDC PUBLISHING

Happy grin

Star-shaped
badge

Lucky shoes

Proud Mood

Chapter One

This is Jack. Today Jack is feeling proud. This week, Jack was chosen as Star of the Week for Most Improved at Reading.

As Star of the Week,
Jack has been picked for
a very special job.

A famous soccer player
is coming to visit Jack's
school this afternoon.
His name is Tim Little.

Jack is going to introduce
Tim Little at assembly.
He is so excited he feels
like he might burst!

Jack and Billie are sitting under the peppercorn tree in the playground.

They are talking about
Tim Little's visit.

"What if I trip on stage?"
Jack worries. "Or mess up
his name?"

Billie giggles. "Imagine
if you accidentally called
him Little Tim," she says.

Jack giggles too. "Or Lim
Tittle!"

The two of them squeal
with laughter.

"I'm so excited!" Jack says.

"Yeah. You're so lucky," Billie says, smiling. "I wish I could meet Tim Little. He's the best!"

Just then the bell goes. Jack feels butterflies flutter in his tummy. There's only a couple more hours until Tim Little is here!

"I'll meet you in the classroom," he tells Billie. "I'm just going to the bathroom."

Jack runs fast so he won't be late for class. Someone is in there washing his hands. It is Aaron.

"Hey, Aaron!" Jack calls.

Then he stops. Aaron's

eyes are red and puffy.

Jack can see he has been

crying. "Are you OK?"

Jack asks.

Aaron nods, but his

mouth scrunches up tight.

"What's the matter?"

Jack asks.

Aaron takes a big breath.

His eyes fill with tears.

"My dog died," he says in

a whisper.

"Oh no," says Jack. "That's terrible!"

"It happened last night," Aaron says. His bottom lip wobbles. "She was very old and sick. Mom says it was time for her to go. But I miss her so much."

Jack understands how Aaron feels. He loves his dog, Scraps.

If Scraps died, Jack would feel awful. Poor Aaron!

Jack puts his arm around Aaron's shoulders. He feels all of Aaron's sadness melt into him.

He wishes he could think of something to cheer him up.

Chapter Two

"Would you like me to walk you back to class?" Jack asks.

Aaron nods. Jack is a bit worried about being late.

But he decides this is an important thing to do. He hopes Ms. Walton will understand.

"Thanks, Jack," Aaron says. "I hope you won't get into trouble for being late."

Jack shrugs. "That's OK," he says. "I don't mind."

They walk along the
hallway together.

"Good luck in assembly
today," Aaron says.

"You're so lucky. I'd love to meet Tim Little. He's awesome!"

"Yeah," says Jack, proudly. Suddenly he has an idea. An awesome idea! He knows just what will cheer Aaron up.

Jack pretends to look worried. "I'm a bit nervous," he says.

"I like Tim Little. But I hate speaking at assembly."

"Really?" says Aaron.

"I don't mind it."

Jack and Aaron arrive at Aaron's classroom door.

"Maybe you could do it instead of me," says Jack. "I'm sure Ms. Walton won't mind."

Aaron's eyes grow very
wide. A huge smile
appears on his face.

"Are you sure? Don't you want to ask someone else, like Billie? Tim Little is her favorite soccer star!"

"Nah," says Jack. "Billie speaks at assembly all the time. If you want to do it, then you should."

"Wow. Thanks, Jack!" Aaron says, laughing. "You're the best."

Jack grins. "I'd better go. Good luck at assembly this afternoon!"

Jack runs down the corridor back to class. He feels a little sad that he won't get to meet Tim Little after all. But he feels a lot happy that he was able to cheer up Aaron.

It must be the worst thing in the world for your dog to die, he thinks.

*I'm sure I can meet someone
famous another time.*

That afternoon, all the students gather in the hall. Everyone is very excited.

It takes the principal, Mrs. Singh, three tries to get them all to be quiet.

Jack sits down next to Billie. She looks surprised.

"Aren't you supposed to be sitting near the stage?" she says. "So you can go up to introduce Tim Little?"

"Aaron is going to do it instead," Jack says.

"You are kidding," Billie says. "It's Tim Little! You might never get the chance to meet someone as famous as him again!"

"That's OK," Jack says, shrugging.

But he feels a worm of worry wriggle in his tummy.

Maybe Billie is right, he thinks. *Maybe I shouldn't have let Aaron do it after all...*

Chapter Three

"OK, quiet down, please," Mrs. Singh says into the microphone. "I know you are all excited to hear from Tim Little today.

Aaron Peters is going to do the introduction."

Some kids twist around to look at Jack. They are confused. Everyone knows it was supposed to be Jack up there. He is Star of the Week, not Aaron. Jack pretends not to notice.

Jack watches Aaron and Tim Little walk onto the stage together. Aaron has a huge grin on his face. He steps up to the microphone. Then he reads out the introduction that Jack wrote. His voice only wobbles a teensy bit.

30

It is a good introduction.

Tim Little shakes Aaron's

hand. Jack smiles.

"Thanks, Aaron, for that great introduction," Tim Little says into the microphone.

The whole school cheers loudly.

"I am here today to talk to you about team spirit," Tim Little says. "Team spirit is about working well in a group. But it is also about being kind and generous to others.

Before this assembly started, Aaron told me about someone who is very kind and generous."

Everybody in the hall starts to murmur and look around. Jack feels his cheeks get hot.

"Aaron told me someone else had been chosen to introduce me today,"

Tim Little says. "But Aaron's dog died last night, so Aaron is very sad.

This other boy knew that Aaron would feel a bit better if he got to meet me today." Tim Little smiles.

"So this boy let Aaron do the introduction. I think this might be one of the kindest things I've ever heard anyone do."

"Wow!" Billie says, smiling at Jack. She squeezes his hand. Jack feels his cheeks get even hotter.

"So, I think it is only right that we have both students up on stage today, don't you?" Tim Little says. "Can everyone please put your hands together for the Star of the Week, Jack Lang!"

Everyone in the hall cheers and claps even louder than before.

Jack stands up. He feels
his legs go wobbly.

Everyone smiles at him as he makes his way to the front. Some kids even reach up to give him a high five as he passes.

Jack is very careful not to fall up the steps. He is very careful not to trip over the microphone cord.

Tim Little holds out a
huge, strong hand for
Jack to shake. Jack's heart
thumps loudly in his ears.

"Thank you, Lim Tittle!" Jack whispers. Then he realizes his mistake. His mouth drops open in horror.

Tim Little snorts with laughter. "No worries, Lack Jang." He winks.

Aaron and Jack both burst into laughter too.

Jack feels so happy. He
made his friend feel better
and met a famous soccer
player. Being Star of the
Week is the best!

Hey Jack! The Crazy Cousins *By Sally Rippin*

Hey Jack! The Scary Solo *By Sally Rippin*

Hey Jack! The Winning Goal *By Sally Rippin*

Hey Jack! The Robot Blues *By Sally Rippin*

Hey Jack! The Worry Monsters *By Sally Rippin*

Hey Jack! The New Friend *By Sally Rippin*

Hey Jack! The Worst Sleepover *By Sally Rippin*

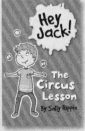
Hey Jack! The Circus Lesson *By Sally Rippin*

Hey Jack! The Bumpy Ride *By Sally Rippin*

Hey Jack! The Top Team *By Sally Rippin*

Hey Jack! The Playground Problem *By Sally Rippin*

Hey Jack! The Best Party Ever *By Sally Rippin*

Hey Jack! The Bravest Kid *By Sally Rippin*

Hey Jack! The Big Adventure *By Sally Rippin*

Hey Jack! The Toy Sale *By Sally Rippin*

Hey Jack! The Star of the Week *By Sally Rippin*

Hey Jack! The Extra-special Group *By Sally Rippin*

Billie B. Brown & Hey Jack! The Book Buddies *By Sally Rippin*

Read them all!
Including a new title starring both Jack AND Billie